JABUTÍ

THE TORTOISE

A TRICKSTER TALE FROM THE AMAZON

TOLD AND ILLUSTRATED BY

Gerald McDermott

Voyager Books
Harcourt, Inc.

Orlando   Austin   New York   San Diego   Toronto   London

For information about permission to reproduce selections from this book, write to trade.permissions@hmhco.com or to Permissions, Houghton Mifflin Harcourt Publishing Company, 3 Park Avenue, 19th Floor, New York, New York 10016.

www.hmhco.com

First Voyager Books edition 2005
Voyager Books is a trademark of Harcourt, Inc., registered in the United States of America and/or other jurisdictions.

The Library of Congress has cataloged the hardcover edition as follows:
McDermott, Gerald.
Jabuti the tortoise: a trickster tale from the Amazon/told and illustrated by Gerald McDermott.
p. cm.
Summary: All the birds enjoy the songlike flute music of Jabuti, the tortoise, except Vulture, who, jealous because he cannot sing, tricks Jabuti into riding his back toward a festival planned by the King of Heaven.
1. Indians of South America—Amazon River Region—Folklore.
2. Tales—Amazon River Region. 3. Turtles—Folklore. [1. Indians of South America—Amazon River Region—Folklore. 2. Folklore—Amazon River Region. 3. Turtles—Folklore. 4. Vultures—Folklore.] I. Title.
F2519.1.A6M33 2001
398.2'09811'0452792—dc21   00-11977
ISBN 0-15-200496-3
ISBN 0-15-205374-3 pb

SCP 22 21 20 19 18
4500775141

The illustrations in this book were done in gouache, colored pencil, and colored ink on 300 lb. hot press Arches watercolor paper.
The display type and text type were set in Neue Neuland Light.
Color separations by Bright Arts Ltd., Hong Kong
Printed and bound by RR Donnelley, China
Production supervision by Ginger Boyer
Typography designed by Lydia D'moch

Jabuti (zha-boo-CHEE) is a central figure in the tribal lore of the Amazon rain forest. Slow and short-legged, the little tortoise is nevertheless portrayed as virtually invincible. Through his cleverness, he is able to overcome larger, often dim-witted foes. These mirthful trickster tales expose human foibles and are enjoyed throughout Brazil.

The first collection of Jabuti stories, from the oral tradition of the Tupi-Guarani and other rain forest tribes, was compiled by Charles Frederick Hartt and published in Rio de Janeiro in 1875 under the title *Os Mitos Amazônicos da Tartaruga.* Since then, the exploits of Jabuti have been retold countless times.

Scholars believe some of the Jabuti stories, like the tales of Brer Terrapin in the southern United States, have a common origin in West Africa. Another cross-cultural link is the King of Heaven, the great god Tupan, who appears throughout the native mythology of the Americas as Thunderbird. The motif of the turtle tumbling from the sky is found in many different traditions, with examples as venerable as Aesop's "The Tortoise and the Eagle," and "The Turtle and the Geese" from the Panchatantra of ancient India.

In the present story, even though Jabuti's world is turned upside down, a universal trickster theme prevails: Creation comes from chaos.

—G. M.

For Tomás and Sofia

Jabuti the tortoise played a song on his flute.
His shell was smooth and shiny, and his song was sweet.

His music wove through the tangled vines and floated above the treetops. All the creatures of the rain forest listened to his song.

For some, Jabutí's song was sour.

Jaguar could remember when Jabutí tricked him into chasing his own tail.

Lizard could remember when Jabutí
tricked him into giving Jabutí a ride on his back.

Tapir could remember when Jabutí
tricked him into a tug-of-war with Whale.

But the birds of the air loved Jabutí's music,
and they sang when he played.

All except Vulture, who could not sing at all.
He was jealous of Jabutí and waited for the
day when he could eat the little tortoise.

There came a time when all the birds of the air were invited to a festival in heaven. The King of Heaven called them together to sing, to rejoice, and to receive his blessing.

When Jabutí saw the great gathering
of the birds, he wanted to go, too.

"I want to play my flute for the King of Heaven," he said. Vulture laughed at him.

"I may not be able to make music like you," said Vulture, "but I can spread my wings and soar all the way to heaven."

"Take me with you," Jabutí pleaded.

Vulture saw his chance.

"Climb on my back, little friend," he said.

Vulture spread his dark wings and rose up in the air. Jabutí held tight to Vulture's feathers as they flew high above the treetops. The dense forest and the great river stretched far below.

They had almost reached heaven when Vulture
suddenly swooped and turned upside down.

Jabutí lost hold of Vulture's feathers
and slipped off his back.

Jabutí went tumbling down through the sky.

The earth came rushing toward him, and he cried out:

> "Twigs and bushes,
> Flowers and trees,
> Move aside,
> Make way for me!"

All the plants and trees of the forest spread apart to make way for Jabutí. But he had forgotten to call to the rock. Jabutí came down on it with a *crack!* and his smooth, shiny shell broke into pieces.

At that moment, the music of the festival in heaven stopped.
The King of Heaven looked down and saw Vulture joining
the other birds.

"Where is Jabuti?" asked the King of Heaven.

Vulture shrugged. "How would I know?" he answered.

"Jabuti wanted to play for me, and you offered to bring him here," said the King of Heaven sternly. "Tell me where he is!"

Vulture turned away from the King of Heaven and hid his head beneath his wing.

The King of Heaven commanded the birds
to search for Jabutí.

The birds filled the sky, flying high over the treetops,
swooping low through the tangled vines,
looking for the little tortoise.

Toucan, Macaw, and Hummingbird found Jabutí.
He was lying helplessly in the forest. His beautiful
shell was broken.

The birds gathered the pieces
and patched him together.

When they were done, Jabutí played a song of thanks for them.

And where the birds had touched Jabutí, they each took on a new color. Toucan got a red and yellow beak, Macaw, bright orange feathers, and Hummingbird, an emerald green belly.

Vulture stayed the same dull color. He still can't sing.

Jabutí the tortoise plays on his flute.
His music weaves through the tangled vines
and floats above the treetops.

His shell may be cracked and patched,
but his song is sweet . . .

at least to some.